READ ALL THE SHARK SCHOOL BOOKS!

Fishin': Impossible

SHARK SCHOOL

 #8 Fishin': Impossible

BY DAVY OCEAN
ILLUSTRATED BY AARON BLECHA

ALADDIN   New York   London   Toronto   Sydney   New Delhi

WiTH THANKS TO PAUL EBBS

ALADDIN

An imprint of Simon & Schuster Children's Publishing Division
1230 Avenue of the Americas, New York, NY 10020
First Aladdin hardcover edition August 2017
Text copyright © 2017 by Hothouse Fiction
Illustrations copyright © 2017 by Aaron Blecha
Also available in an Aladdin paperback edition.
All rights reserved, including the right of reproduction in whole or in part in any form.
ALADDIN and related logo are registered trademarks of Simon & Schuster, Inc.
For information about special discounts for bulk purchases, please contact
Simon & Schuster Special Sales at 1-866-506-1949 or business@simonandschuster.com.
The Simon & Schuster Speakers Bureau can bring authors to your live event. For more
information or to book an event contact the Simon & Schuster Speakers Bureau at 1-866-248-3049
or visit our website at www.simonspeakers.com.
Jacket designed by Karin Paprocki
Interior designed by Mike Rosamilia
The text of this book was set in Write Demibd.
Manufactured in the United States of America 0617 FFG
2 4 6 8 10 9 7 5 3 1
Library of Congress Control Number 2016959296
ISBN 978-1-4814-6550-2 (hc)
ISBN 978-1-4814-6549-6 (pbk)
ISBN 978-1-4814-6551-9 (eBook)

CHAPTER 1

"OWWWWooooooooOWWWWWooooo-
ooWWWWWOOOOOOOOOWWWWWoo-
oooooOWWWWWoooooooWWWWW-
OOOOOOOOOWWWWooooooooO-
WWWWWoooooo!!!!!!!!!!"

Let me explain.

That is the sound of me being swung by the tail.

Yes. Tail.

I'm a hammerhead shark. Which means I have a hammer-shaped head at one end, and a tail at the other. Which means I'm the dorkiest-looking shark there is, ever, in the history of shark (and that goes way, way, way back).

"Oooowwwwwwwwwwwwwwwwww-
wwwwwwwww!!!!!!"

And that's the sound of me flying across the school playground, over the heads, fins, and tentacles of the other kids and squids.

I bounce on the finball field straight into the goal, bulging in the net like a leggy air-breather's catch.

I guess you want to know why this is happening to me.

As I lie here upside down, and feeling more than a little inside out, I'm asking myself the very same question.

But before I can find a proper answer, I'm being dragged out of the goal by my friends Tony the Tiger Shark and Ralph the Pilot Fish.

"Wow!" says Tony, turning me the right way up.

"Double wow!" says Ralph, straightening my school blazer and glancing into my mouth. He's trying to see if my crash landing has dislodged any leftover breakfast from my teeth. Ralph is a pilot fish, and pilot fish love eating leftover food from sharks' teeth. That might seem gross to you leggy air-breathers, but to me it's the best way of having my teeth cleaned. At least I don't have to do it half asleep at the mirror while my mom moans at me about the state of my bedroom.

So why was I being spun around and thrown through the sea like a rubber-headed javelin made of shark? It's because the sea-circus has come to town and we all went last night. It was *great*.

MY TOP FOUR SEA-CIRCUS ACTS

1. The Seahorse Riders . . . tiny krill jockeys performing epic tricks on the backs of furiously finning seahorses

2. The Krazy Clownfishes . . . who ride around in a wobbly multicolored submarine. It falls apart every time they beep the horn. Hilarious!

3. The beautiful Trapseas Artists . . . who swing from the roof of the circus tent on sequined, driftwood trapseases

4. But best of all, the act we really love the most . . . are the Acrosprats!

Tumbling across the circus ring, fin flipping and flip finning, the Acrosprats are so strong, even their scales have muscles. They climb poles, balance on one another's dorsals, and spin one another by the tails to fly at other Acrosprats zooming in from the other side of the tent!

They look as if they're going to *crash* headfirst into the other Acrosprats in a massive *smash* of scales and gills! But at the last second they just manage to twist out of the way. That's the move Ralph and Tony just tried with me, which was why I was sent flying

across the playground into the goal.

We'd all been so blown away by the Acrosprats last night that we couldn't wait to try out some of their moves ourselves. Well, when I say *all*, I mean all of my friends apart from Joe the Jellyfish. He just covered his eyes with his sixteen tentacles and bottom-popped with anxiety. He bottom-pops with anxiety a lot because he spends most of his time more scared than an octopus in a piranha school. (For those of you who don't know, piranhas are the bite-iest, nibbliest fish in the ocean.)

Luckily no one was trying the same

trick from the other direction. I wouldn't have had a chance of getting out of the way—I was too busy trying not to be sick from all those somersaults.

So when this next thing happens . . .

Flub-b-b-b-b-b-b-b-b-b-b-b-b-b-b-b-b-b-b-b-b-b-b-b-b-b-e-r!!!!!!

It really doesn't help at all.

"Howdy, ice-pick face!"

It's Rick Reef, my reef-shark enemy and the school bully. He's finned up behind me and *whacks* one end of my hammer with his tail. My hammer head vibrates like a ruler *twanged* on the edge of a school desk.

It takes a while for my head to clear because *flubbering* rattles my googly eyes around like socks in a clothes dryer. When I finally get my vision back to normal, Rick is showing off to everyone around me. He's holding a clamshell notebook and showing all the watergraphs he got backstage at the sea-circus last night!

Every single Acrosprat has signed the book!

"But I didn't just get their watergraphs!" Rick says smugly. "The Acrosprats gave me a couple of tumbling lessons too— look!"

Rick throws the notebook to Donny Dogfish, his dumb-as-a-shark's-rear-end sidekick. Then he takes off, zooming into the currents above our heads. The zippers on his black leather jacket glint in the greeny sea-light.

Once Rick's high above us, he starts doing forward nose-rolls, and twists into a crazy tail-flick-flack. It looks as if he's tying himself into a knot but then he comes out the other side, sliding into five dorsal-jumps and an awesome snapper-shank. His grin is so big, we can see all his teeth, and he flings his fins wide open.

The kids and squids watching go crazy clapping and cheering.

I nudge Ralph and Tony. "Quick! Swing me around! Make me go higher and farther than last time. Rick's not the only one who can do acrospratics!"

"But . . . ," says Ralph.

I flap my tail over his mouth. *"Now!"* I bark.

Ralph and Tony look at each other and shrug. Then they grab the end of my tail and swing me around as hard and as fast as they can.

I hear Rick and Donny laughing as I spin around and around. But I don't care. This'll show everyone that Rick isn't the only one who can bust some moves!

Except . . .

Joe bottom-pops the biggest pop I've ever heard. Ralph and Tony start choking and coughing.

"Awwwwwwwwww, Joe! That smells worse than a rotting fish head stuck inside a walrus's armpit!" Tony yells. He and Ralph are coughing so hard they let go of me.

They let go of me too soon and . . .

"Waaaaaaaaaaaaaaaaaaaaaaaaaaaaaaaaa-
aaaaaaaaaaaaaaaaaaaaahhhhhhhhhhhhhh-
hhhhhhhhhhhhhhhhhhhhhhhhhh!!!!!"

I'm flying backward against the current. I'm twisting like an eel plugged into a light socket. I'm crashing face-first into *Rick*!!!!!!

Rick and I tumble end over tail.

My fins are in a tangle.

My mouth is full of Rick's jacket.

I can feel my teeth ripping into it, tearing a gaping hole in the side!

When we finally skid to a halt against one of the playground garbage cans, I have a mouthful of leather and a zipper is hanging off the end of my hammer. There's also a Rick-shaped volcano about to explode.

"*Sowwwwy.*" (That's me trying to say "Sorry" but all I manage to do is spit leather and a couple of teeth at him.)

Volcano Rick erupts. And goes straight for my head, again and again and again.

Flllllllluuuuuuuubbbbbbbeeeeerrrrrrrrrr-rrrrrrrrrrrrrr!!!!

"You goofball!"

Flllllllluuuuuuuubbbbbbbeeeeerrrrrrrrrr-rrrrrrrrrrrrrr!!!!

"That's my best jacket!!!"

Flllllllluuuuuuuubbbbbbbeeeeerrrrrrrrrr-rrrrrrrrrrrrrr!!!!

"I'm going to *flubber* you from here into the middle of next week!!!!"

Flllllluuuuuuuubbbbbbeeeeerrrrrrrrr-rrrrrrrrrrrrrr!!!!

And he does.

Flllllluuuuuuuuubbbbbbeeeeerrrrrrrrr-rrrrrrrrrrrrrr!!!!

Well . . .

Flllllluuuuuuuuubbbbbbeeeeerrrrrrrrr-rrrrrrrrrrrrrr!!!!

It's more like the middle of next *month.*

Flllllluuuuuuuuubbbbbbeeeeerrrrrrrrr-rrrrrrrrrrrrrr!!!!

CHAPTER 2

I manage to make it through the rest of the school day with Rick only throwing evil stares at me, but I bet he'd rather be throwing desks and chairs.

I keep my mouth shut and take it, counting down the seconds till school's over.

When I finally get home I swim straight

up to my room and throw myself on my
seabed.

I'm mad.

Really mad.

As usual, Humphrey my humming-fish
alarm clock and Larry my lantern-fish
lamp are no help at all.

"Awwww look at his little face," says Humphrey.

"Sadder than a swordfish gone blunt," says Larry.

"More miserable than a crab who can't walk sideways," says Humphrey.

I ignore them and take out my journal and begin to write.

A LIST OF ALL THE REASONS I HATE RICK REEF

1.   He's a flippering show-off!!!!

2.   He's always trying to do things better than me!!!

3.   He makes me look fin-diculous in front of girls!!!

4. He keeps FLUBBERING my flippering HAMMER!!!

5. I WISH I'D NEVER MET HIM!!!

6. I WISH HE'D MOVE AWAY FROM SHARK POINT TONIGHT.

7. He totally ruined my circus act!

But writing the list just makes me more miserable. I seriously wish the ocean floor would open up right now and *swallow me whole*!!!!!

"Oh, Harry-Warry!!!!"

Great. Now Mom's calling me. I ignore her.

"Harry-Warry! You might want to come downstairs."

21

No, I really might not. I might want to sit up here and sulk.

"Have you seen the time Harry-Warry?" Humphrey shows me his clock face. "Huh?"

"It's time for *Mike Hammerhead, Shark Detective*!" Mom calls.

MIKE HAMMERHEAD, SHARK DETECTIVE!!!!

My favorite program on telefishion! My number one hero—after Gregor the Gnasher!

I immediately forget my sulk and leap from my seabed. I rush past Humphrey and Larry, sending them spinning away in my wake, and I zoom downstairs as fast as my fins will carry me.

"On the mean seas, you have to be meaner than mean," Mike Hammerhead booms from the telefishion.

I crunch down on a finful of wet-roasted

seanuts in the meanest way possible.
Dad snorts.

Mike Hammerhead pulls up the collar
on his coat. *"If you stop swimming, the
bad guys will only swim faster."*

I chew faster. Dad sighs as he flicks

through pages on his octopiPad looking for pictures of himself. He's Mayor of Shark Point and loves being in the news. Sadly, he doesn't love *Mike Hammerhead, Shark Detective.*

I think it's The. Best. Most. Exciting. And. Greatest. Show. *Ever!!! And* Mike Hammerhead's a hammerhead. Double win!

But Dad just thinks it's awful.

"I knew the statue of the Maltese Parrot Fish was a fake all along," Mike Hammerhead says as he swims into some spooky-looking docks. *"And I knew how to prove it. But now someone's try-ing to silence me for keeps. The Lobster*

Mobsters are gonna send me to the sur-face in a concrete lobster pot!"

"I wish they would, you ridiculous excuse for a hammerhead!" Dad huffs.

"Dad! I'm trying to watch this!"

But Dad's not listening. "I don't know why you bother with this show, Harry." He keeps flicking on his octopiPAD. "If Mike Hammerhead was a real detective he wouldn't be able to detect what was stuck down the back of the fridge, let alone find the Maltese Parrot Fish!"

I almost choke on a finful of seanuts. "Dad, I can't hear what he's saying!"

On the screen, three mega-mean

lobsters with steel-tipped claws are backing Mike Hammerhead into a corner.

"*You've been sticking your hammer where it's not wanted!*" the head lobster drawls.

"Well, it's certainly not wanted around here!"

"Dad!"

I chew even faster as the mega-mean lobsters threaten Mike Hammerhead with their razor-sharp claws.

Mike Hammerhead reaches into his pocket. "*No one tells me where to stick my hammer!*" he yells as he pulls his Seaberry smartphone from his pocket.

He flicks on the camera and it flashes bright white light in the lobsters' eyes!

The lobsters groan and writhe, trying to cover their eye-stalks with the claws that only moments before were going to chop Mike into shark sushi!

Mike slips from their grasp, pulls a huge fishing net from a nearby boat, and throws it over them!

As the lobsters yell and tangle themselves up in the net, Mike calls the police on his phone, telling them that the bad guys have been caught. Then he looks straight at the camera and delivers his famous catchphrase. *"Sometimes justice is left to just us."*

Great!

I look at Dad. His eyes are shiny with excitement. He *does* like Mike Hammerhead—he just doesn't want to admit it! I'm about to say something when he notices me looking at him. He buries his nose back in his octopiPAD with a harrumph.

Classic!

Back in my room I float onto my bed, imagining how cool it must be to be a shark detective . . . catching criminals, getting into danger and finding missing treasure.

29

I reckon I'd make a great detective when I grow up. Or some kind of cool secret agent. And that's something Rick could never do. He's nowhere near smart enough.

I reach out a fin for my diary to add *He's so dumb* to my list of reasons why I hate Rick. But the space on top of my bedside crabinet is empty.

I look up. The journal isn't there!

I look down. The journal isn't there!

I look under my seabed. The journal isn't there!

"There must have been an intruder!" I imagine Mike Hammerhead saying.

I leap into action.

"Humphrey!" I shout, pulling Larry off the shelf where he'd been sleeping. I press his nose to turn on his light. Humphrey swims down off the wall where he'd been ticking quietly, reading a comic. "What's up?" he says, looking confused. "It's not time to set your alarm, is it?"

I swing Larry around by the tail, pointing him right in Humphrey's face. I saw
Mike Hammerhead doing this with a suspect last week. It was a great interroga-
tion technique. Humphrey's face lights
up and his eyes go all squinty. "Who's
been in this room?" I ask.

"Me," Humphrey says.

I sigh. "Who else?"

"You."

I squeeze Larry's tail and his light
becomes brighter. I repeat something Mike
Hammerhead said last week when he was
interviewing a prime suspect. "Don't play
Sally Silent with me, you stoolie."

32

Humphrey looks confused. "Can you say that again in Fin-glish? I have no idea what you're talking about. . . ."

I feel Larry shaking with laughter in my fin. I turn him around to give him a menacing stare . . . and I'm blinded by his light!

I let Larry go so that I can rub my eyes. He swims around, giggling and high-finning Humphrey.

When the dazzle fades and I can see the room again, I do what I should have done in the first place. I turn on my hammer-vision and almost immediately see the corner of my diary sticking over the side of the shelf where Larry had been sitting.

"You did this!" I yell as I swim up to the shelf and retrieve the diary. I see right away that it's open where I'd made my list about Rick—and I also see that Humphrey and Larry have been writing something against every entry! LOOK!!!!

A LIST OF ALL THE REASONS I HATE RICK REEF

1. He's a flippering show-off!!!! *(Oh, you never try to show off, do you? Not!)*

2. He's always trying to do things better than me!!! *(And you never try to do things better than Rick, do you? Not!)*

3. He makes me look fin-diculous in front of girls!!! *(Well to be fair, you're much better at that than Rick is.)*

4. He keeps FLUBBERING my flippering HAMMER!!! *(And so do you. Especially when you crash into things, trying to do number 1 and number 2 on your list. Hahahaha!)*

5. I WISH I'D NEVER MET HIM!!! *(Well if you'd never met him, who would you make silly lists about?!!!!)*

6. I WISH HE'D MOVE AWAY FROM SHARK POINT TONIGHT. *(We agree with you there!)*

7. He totally ruined my circus act! *(Didn't you do that all on your own?)*

Humphrey and Larry clutch their stomachs with their fins as they float around laughing.

Grrrrrrrrrrrrrrrrrrrrrrrrrrrrrrrrrrrrrrrrrrrrrrrrrrrrrrrrrrrrrrrrrrrrrrrrrrrrrrrrr!!!!

"I'm going to *bed*!!!" I shout. I pull the seaweed covers over my hammer and stuff my fins into my ears to shut out their laughter.

CHAPTER 3

"Mmmahamhamahammmamamamah-hhhh."

"What?"

"Mmmahamhamahammmamamamah-hhhh."

"What?" I wriggle around and look at my friend Tony the Tiger Shark.

"I said, can you get your tail out of my mouth!?!?" he splutters.

"Oh right." I push down on his shoulder. "Okay, flip me over!"

Tony flips me. I fly, twist, crash into Ralph, and bounce into Joe, who pops from one end and burps from the other. "Ouch!" he yelps. "Jellyfish are not good at being squished!"

We've been trying some more Acrosprat moves on the way to school today, and I'm determined that Rick isn't going to get all the attention this time. If I get enough practice in, everyone will be cheering *me*.

"Come on, then!" I shout at the others.

But Tony is rubbing his fin and Ralph is rubbing his head and neither of them look happy.

"Give it a rest, Harry," says Ralph. "I'm fed up with my head being a landing pad for your acrospratics!"

Tony, Ralph, and the ever-popping Joe swim on toward school. I follow behind feeling even worse than I did yesterday.

When we get to school there's a buzzing crowd of kids around the gate. Our teacher, Mrs. Shelby, is there too, which is really weird. Normally she'd already be in class. Mrs. Shelby bangs a ship's nail on her shell and all the kids fall silent.

We swim up, wafting our fins as quietly as we can. I keep half an eye out for Rick just in case he somersaults over the crowd doing three perfect fin-bombs to land perfectly on my hammer and *flubber* me.

"Children, please listen carefully," Mrs. Shelby says. "You may have noticed that Rick Reef isn't in the playground this morning. I'm afraid he won't be in school at all today."

Yes! I have to try really hard not to swim a celebratory lap of the school field, chucking in a few fin-bombs as I go.

Then Mrs. Shelby spoke so quietly we could barely hear her. "It's my sad duty to inform you," she whispered, "that Rick Reef disappeared last night."

Pop! Pop! Pop!

That anxious bottom-popping isn't Joe.

It's me. *I've* just popped!

Don't tell anyone.

"Rick left a note with his parents telling them that he's swum away to join the sea-circus," Mrs. Shelby explains. "The circus has now moved on to Wreck Reef. Apparently Rick wants to become an Acrosprat."

Pearl and Cora the dolphin twins look at each other and gasp.

"But I can reassure you that Rick's mother and father, along with Officer Robert Eel of the Shark Point Police Department, are on their way to pick him up right now. And they will be taking him straight home."

Typical! Not only has Rick gotten himself a whole day at the sea-circus, he's wrangled himself a day off from school!

So not fair.

I wish I'd thought of that.

The morning classes are full of excited whispering about Rick and how brave he was to swim away from home like that.

I'm not excited at all. I'm mad. Rick's managed to be the center of attention all day *without even being here*!

At break time Tony and Ralph still don't want to practice any moves. All they want to do is play boring old finball. How are we going to become Acrosprats by doing that? We can't all run away and join the circus.

Joe doesn't want to play finball—the ball scares him too much. He only wants to talk about Rick. "I really hope his parents get to him before he gets trapped in the sea lion taming cage," he says.

"Huh?"

"Well, those sea lions can be vicious and nasty. But it's not just them that are dangerous."

"No?"

"No. If he's not careful he might get

knocked unconscious by the Krazy-Clownfish submarine blowing apart when they're rehearsing and be trampled by a rampaging stampede of sea horses scared by the noise. You never know."

"Joe." I ask, "Do you really believe all of that could happen?"

"Yes, Harry. The sea is a danger-ous place, really dangerous, and the sea-circus is at least three times as dangerous."

45

"Thank you," I tell him, finning him on the back.

"What are you thanking me for? I've just told you about all the horrible things that could have happened to Rick."

"I know," I say. "And you've really cheered me up!"

On my way home from school, I let Ralph, Tony, and Joe go on ahead. They're still more interested in finball or being doomy and gloomy about every silly little thing and wondering about Rick. But why would I waste time

on Rick when I can be thinking about *Mike Hammerhead, Shark Detective*?

My favorite ever episode was on last year. In it, Mike was in a strange town a long way from home. He was on the trail of a desperate gang of squidnappers who'd taken the richest squid in the ocean, Krill Gates, the creator of Findows 10, to a secret hideaway, and they wanted his company to pay them a huge ransom or he'd never be seen again!

I imagined I was Mike Hammerhead, slinking in the shadows, sneaking down the deserted streets of an unknown town. Staying out of the streetlights, ducking down

below windows, turning corners slowly, just sticking a smidge of hammer-eye out to look first, not sure who was an enemy and who was a friend, swimming down alleyways, being *smart*, being mean, being *Mike Hammerhead, Shark Detective!!!!*

Yeah.

I think that's when I got a bit lost.

I shake my head clear of my Mike Hammerhead daydream and look around.

Uh-oh . . . I have absolutely no idea where I am!

The streets are unfamiliar. I swim ahead a little bit and that's when I see that I'm at an end of Shark Point known as the Shallows.

The water is brighter here because we're nearer the surface. Hardly any sea creatures come here because it's too close to the leggy air-breathers who are always trying to catch us. I really should turn around and go back . . . and try to find home. But . . .

Hang on.

What's that?

Something black is snagged on a rock up ahead. As I swim toward it through the warm water, it catches a glint of sunlight.

A *zipper*!

When I reach the rock I can't believe my eyes.

It's Rick's leather jacket!

My teeth marks are still on it and the zipper I ripped out is still missing! There's no way Rick would have left his precious jacket here, not even with the holes. Everyone knows he loves that jacket.

My mind races. What does this mean?

If Rick really went off to join the sea-circus *why* would his jacket be here?

I don't like the gurgling feelings this is making in my tummy.

I'm scared. But I'm even more scared for Rick! When I wrote in my diary that I wished I'd never met him I didn't mean it. Not really. I'm sure it's been character-building knowing him. And every hero needs a nemesis, right? I look around the empty water, unsure what to do.

What would Mike Hammerhead do if he found a clue like this?

"Even if you don't like the guy, and the guy clearly doesn't like you and flips

your flubber every other second, you have to save him, Harry," I imagine Mike Hammerhead saying. And he's right! I've no choice. *"Sometimes justice is left to just us."*

I pick up the jacket. I can't go back home to Shark Point now. I have to see if Rick is up ahead!

I swim on slowly, keeping the jacket hugged close to my chest. After a minute or so I can hear something.

Is it the sound of the waves breaking on the shore?

"On the mean shore you have to be sure you're going in the right direction,"

says Imaginary Mike Hammerhead in my hammery head.

I realize that the sound isn't waves breaking, it's cheering! Lots of leggy air-breathers cheering and applauding and laughing!

Should I go on?

"*When the stakes are high, don't get made into shark steaks.*" Hmm, not quite so helpful, Imaginary Mike!

Up ahead I see where the cheering is coming from. A huge see-through enclosure is reaching down from the beach into the Shallows. Hundreds

and hundreds and *hundreds* of leggy air-breathers are sitting around it. Way more than I've ever seen before because I've never been this close to the land before! They all seem to be having a great time.

Splash!!!!!

A dolphin drops into the enclosure and the crowd goes wild!

Splash!!!! Splasssssssssssssh!!!!!

Two more slither in and start racing around the edge of the pool.

Through the shallow water I can see them flicking their tails and sending huge sprays of water over the leggy air-breathers.

Then the three dolphins race up to the surface, explode from the water, do three double-nose-ends and a side-flack, and then *ker-splash*!!!!! Back into the water!

The crowd rises from their chairs, yelling with delight, cheering and stamping their weird feety things.

Those dolphins are not that good, I think to myself. *That side-flack was nowhere near as radical as the one I can do. I bet I could—*

But before I can think, another disaster strikes: From out of nowhere *a huge net* scoops me up and lifts me right *out of the sea!!!!!!!!!!*

CHAPTER 4

"When the bad guys' net is closing, you don't wanna be around to get caught!"

Er, bit late for that, Imaginary Mike. Like, seriously late! Don't you have better advice than that?

I'm blinded by the sunlight as I'm pulled from the sea. I hold my gill water (like you leggy air-breathers hold your breath) and try to figure out what just happened.

Blinking in the sunlight I see that I'm in a large net, hanging from the end of a crane arm. The crane is on a boat and the boat is heading for what I think is the shore!

My googly-eyes start bulging and my chest aches. I won't be able to hold the gill water for much longer.

The crane starts to swing and as I look down I see the enclosure where the dolphins are doing their tricks. There's a smaller, water-filled tank next to it. I'm being taken toward it.

"Attention! Attention!" an amplified leggy air-breather's voice booms from below. "If all visitors care to look up to the crane swinging into the Sea-Planet Theme Park right now, you'll see our latest attraction. A hammerhead shark!"

They're talking about me!

I look around as we clank nearer, seeing thousands of leggy air-breathers, roller coasters, rides, aquariums, ice-cream stands, and there—right below me—one huge pool where the dolphins are performing (and looking like they're getting royally annoyed because every-one is looking at me and pointing) and beyond that a smaller-looking, gloomier pool. It's the smaller pool I seem to be heading for.

The idea terrifies me. A theme park? What are they going to make me do???????

My gills are bursting. All I can hear is my heartbeat thudding in my ears and the *clanking* of the crane as it swings me across the dolphin's pool.

"When you're up to your neck in the—"

Shut it, Mike! *Shut it!!!!*

Cllannnnnnnnnnnnnnnnnnnnnnngggg!!!

Ziiiiiiiiiiippppp!!!!

Ker-splash!!!!!!!!!!!!!!!!!!!!!!!!!!!!!!!!!!

That's the crane thudding to a halt, the net being opened, and me falling into the smaller pool.

The water here is a bit murky, and tastes funny, but at least it's water. And it's great being able to breathe properly again.

I can just make out the far wall through the gloom, so it's not a very big pool. About three times the size of Mrs. Shelby's classroom, I reckon. The bottom isn't the seafloor I'm used to—it's white tiles covered with swirls of dirty sand.

It's not a very nice place to be, and I shiver.

I don't like it at all.

Then I look behind me.

"Arrrrrrrrrrrrrrrrggggggggggggggggggg-hhhhhhhhh!!!"

I swim back fast and *thump* hard into the wall behind me.

You will not believe what I saw!

There are a lot of leggy air-breathers, just standing there looking at me! Some are pointing, some are laughing, and some are looking bored and picking their noses and gazing up at their moms and dads.

How can they be here in the water with me?

Leggy air-breathers are as useless underwater as I am in the air. They can't breathe down here.

Except . . .

They do look a bit . . . *weird.*

As I get my breath back and my heart calms down, I realize that the leggy air-breathers aren't in the water with me. They're *behind* glass!

I swim forward, cautiously.

The laughing, the pointing, and the bored nose-picking increases.

My hammer bumps gently against the glass.

Boink.

The nearest leggy air-breather kid jumps back and grabs his mom.

"Let me out! I don't wanna be in your stupid Sea-Planet Theme Park!" I yell,

finning hard on the glass. "Please, let me go back to the ocean!"

They can't hear me, or don't care what I'm saying. All they want to do is look at me.

"You can't talk to them, idiot face," a voice says behind me. "Just how stupid are you?"

What?!

I spin around and, there, approaching slowly out of the gloom, is Rick!!!

That's right, Rick Reef!

"What-what are you doing here?" I stammer.

"What does it look like, toolbox head? I've been captured, just like you!"

"No way!"

"Yes way."

I look back at the leggy air-breathers, peering at us through the glass. "What are they going to do to us?"

"How should I know? Feed us to the leggy air-breather lions?"

I really don't like the idea of that.

Rick goes on. "Or maybe they're just going to keep us in here so they can stare at us like dorks?"

I really don't like the idea of being trapped in here with Rick for the rest of my life either.

"Great," Rick mutters. "Trapped in a giant goldfish bowl with a giant toolbox for company!"

I realize I still have his leather jacket tucked up under my fin. I hold it out to him. "I actually came looking for you when I found this on the rocks outside. I knew there was no way in the ocean you'd leave your precious jacket any-where. But the first thing you do when I get here is call me names. I wish I hadn't bothered." I shake it at him. "Go on. Take it. I'm not carrying it around anymore."

Rick takes the jacket and for a moment I think I see a smile appear on his jaws. "You came looking for me?"

"Yes. I thought you might be in danger."

Rick frowns. "I didn't think you'd care if I was in danger."

"Well, if you didn't spend so much time *flubbering* my hammer you might have found out."

Rick puts on his jacket and his smile grows. "Whatever, I'm just glad I have this back."

We fin over to the back of the tank so that the leggy air-breathers can't see us through the gloom. I'm really creeped out by all those faces watching us.

"So, what happened?" I ask him. "I thought you'd gone off to join the sea-circus?"

"Mom and Dad wouldn't let me go to the sea-circus again. I really wanted to see the Acrosprats bust a few more moves." Rick sighs. "They're so cool, man. But Mom said I had to stay in and do my homework. She's so unreasonable. So I swam out my bedroom window, and since it's like *miles* to Wreck Reef, and I wanted to get there before dark, I took a shortcut through the Shallows and was scooped up just like you."

Rick points through the murky water to the leggy air-breathers. "And that group has been watching my every move since I got here. I can't believe they'd come here just to watch me and you swimming around being miserable. What kind of creatures would want to do that?"

I decide not to point out to Rick that he likes to spend quite a lot of time making me miserable so that he can watch me and laugh. There's no point getting into an argument when we're both in a mess.

"We need to find a way out," I say. I can't bear the thought of never seeing Mom and Dad again—or Ralph and my friends. We need to get out of here before they come looking for us. There's no way I want them getting caught here too.

"It's not gonna happen, Harry. You think I haven't tried? The sides are too high above the surface of the water and we're too far from the shore to swim it even if we did get out."

"Be smarter. Think harder," Imaginary Mike Hammerhead says in my head.

"There will be a way out, Rick, we just have to think."

"You've seen the solution to the crime already, you just haven't understood it yet. That's the trick to being a great detective. Turning seeing into understanding. . . ."

Think. Think. If I've seen it all already . . . what does he mean?

Ping!!! I turn on my hammer-vision and

use the replay function to watch my crane journey in the net: up out of the sea, up over the pool where the dolphins were performing. I use hammer-vision zoom, to focus on the end of the dolphin pool nearest the sea and . . .

Yes!!!!!!!!!!!!!!!!!!!

Imaginary Mike Hammerhead is right! I've seen the solution *already*!!! There is a way out. There really is! I hunch my shoulders like I'm pulling my imaginary raincoat up, and pretend to tip my imaginary hat.

I knew I had it in me to be a super special undercover agent detective!

This time I do hug Rick! I throw my fins around him and begin to dance.

"I've cracked it! I've flippering *cracked it*! We can escape, and I know exactly how!!!!!"

CHAPTER 5

Rick wriggles out of the hug and fins me away. "Get off me, mallet head!"

But I'm too excited to be annoyed by his latest insult. I have a plan. "Listen to me, Rick, I think I know how we can get out of here."

"Yeah, right."

"*When everyone is telling you you're wrong, remember, you might be right.*"

Yes, Imaginary Mike! Yes!

"Rick, when you were being hauled into here in the net, what did you see?"

"My backside. I was bent in half. I think I sprained my swim bladder."

"*You have to notice everything. Great detectives don't get to be great just looking at their backsides.*"

I wish I could show Rick the things I *noticed* as I was being lifted in by the crane, but Rick doesn't have hammer-vision replay. If Rick was a hammerhead like me, I could have at least *Blueshark-Toothed*

the replay to him, but Rick's a reef shark. I'm going to have to show him what the hammer-vision showed me. For real.

"Rick," I say. "Come with me!"

I drag Rick up by the fin until we head for the surface.

"Faster!" I shout, encouraging him to kick his tail harder. "Imagine you're going for the sickest triple gill of all time."

"Why?"

"Just do it!"

We both kick harder and harder. Rick lets go of my fin, shooting waveward, and I'm only a split-second behind.

Fwoooooooooooooooooooooooooooosh!!!!!

We break surface! As we shoot up into air, I point to the pool beyond ours, where I saw the dolphins doing their junky tricks. "What can you see?"

"The ocean, too far away!"

We're still rising, but we'll reach the top of our jump in a moment and start to fall back, "No! Nearer! *Look!*"

As we start to fall back, I point and Rick looks, "The next pool over, it dips right down into the ocean!" he says.

"Yes!" I shout as the wave tops of our pool start to get closer. "If we can get into that pool, I bet we have a good chance of jumping over that wall, and escaping."

80

Plashhhhhhhhhhhhhh!!! (That's Rick.)

Ploooooooooooooooooooooooooshhh!!!
(That's me.)

And we're back in our pool.

"Are you sure?"

I nod my hammer. "Yes! I know I can jump it, and you've always been able to jump higher than me. I reckon we have a *great* chance!"

Rick frowns. "Hmm. If it's that easy how come the dolphins haven't gotten over the wall and swam away?"

"Dolphins love doing tricks. You've seen them at Shark Point always show-ing off. Maybe if they get a chance to do tricks all day they take it. They probably love leggy air-breathers too. They're crazy like that."

"Yeah, right," Rick snorts. "They love being kept prisoner here. They love the leggy air-breathers staring at them all the time."

"Well, that's what happens in theme parks like Sea-Planet I guess. Anyway, the dolphins aren't our problem. We are our problem."

"*You* are *my* problem, you mean."

"All right, what's *your* plan, then?" I ask him huffily.

"I don't have one."

I feel like screaming at Rick.

"Cool it, kid. Great detectives never take out their frustrations on sea-villians. No one can detect the stuff we do. Only we have hammer-vision. True, or true?"

Okay, Mike, okay. True.

It takes two deep gills to calm me down.

"Sooooo, if I have a plan and you don't, my plan has to be worth a shot, right?"

Rick thinks and his eyes bug out while he does it. Thinking looks like it hurts him. A lot. Eventually he nods. "I guess so," Rick says, looking like his eyes are going to slide off the side of his face.

"*See? He kinda gets it. But you had better make double sure though, kid. You don't want this plan sliding out of his head like earwax in a hot ocean.*"

Ewwwwwwwwwwwwwwwwwwwwww.

I fin-bump Rick and begin Operation Explain the Escape.

FIN BUMP

I lead Rick around our tiny pool, past the ogling leggy air-breathers, around and around, at the same time explaining to him what we have to do.

When I'm sure he has it, I fly up—*sploooolshing* out of the water for a fin-flack while Rick *thwoooooshes* into four nose-ends and a tail-gimbal below me.

It's all going really well until . . .

Crrrrrrrrrunch!!!!

Thud!!!

Rick flips into me, upends me by the tail, and sends me sprawling against the glass. The leggy air-breathers laugh and point.

I float there for a moment. Stunned.

"Kid, kid. I reckon if you swap—"

I know, Mike! I know!

Once I've caught my breath, I swim back toward Rick. "Okay. Okay. You do the fin-flack, I'll do the gimbal. Okay?"

Rick nods reluctantly.

"We have to show them we're the greatest, Rick. We have to be the best!!!"

This time the move is pulled off perfectly, and Rick flies up above the surface of the tank and splashes down with a perfect star-splash.

"Great," I shout. "Again!"

We dive and we leap and we splash

86

up and down. We're all fins and tails and snappy teeth.

Move.

After move.

After *move*!!!

We're the champion Acrosprats of this tank.

I push Rick up with my hammer, he twists into the sunlight, bursting from the water, yelling like we've just won the Finball World Cup!

The crowd of leggy air-breathers grows bigger and bigger, pressing their noses against the glass.

Yes! This is exactly what I wanted!!

"Again!" I call to Rick as I power up another twisting cartfluke and double splish-frazzle.

Rick leaps over me in a sick triple-turning overbite, catching hold of my fin as he goes, swinging me up into a radical dorsal-slash with a totally hairy bottom-lunge. It's like we're really in the sea-circus!

Faster and faster we swim and I'm desperately hoping the leggy air-breathers who run Sea-Planet will see how fantastic we are. So fantastic that they'll no longer want us in the ridiculously tiny pool, but will want us in the main performance area!

"It's a longship kid, a real longship."

I know it's a risk, Mike. I know. But you take risks all the time when you're on a case, don't you?

"I do, kid. So go for it. I reckon you have this licked!"

Clang!!!

Yes. *Yes!! Yesssss!!!!* A huge shadow moves above us. My risky plan is working! I knew the leggy air-breathers couldn't resist us! It's why they caught us in the first place!

The crane is swinging over the tank and the net is being lowered into the water. "Swim into it," I tell Rick.

Rick stares at me. "Are you crazy?"

"Just do it!"

I power into the net, hold it open for Rick and beckon him in.

Eventually, after probably deciding that he doesn't want to be left in the tank all alone, he swims in.

The crane clanks and squeaks. The net is dragged up. "Hold your gill-water, Rick!" I yell as we break through the sur-face of the ocean.

And then we're out in the light holding our gills as hard as we can.

The crane swings toward the dolphin's pool . . .

And we're dropped right in.

Ker-splash!!!!

Ker-splash!!!!

My plan worked!!!!

The water here is much cleaner and fresher because it's coming directly from the sea. Above the waves I can see the faces of all the leggy air-breathers sitting around expectantly—waiting for us to begin our show.

"No show, kid, no show. You have a jailbreak to attend to."

Right on, Mike. Right on.

"Come on, Rick, let's get out of here!"

I swim as fast as I can toward the sea,
looking over the wall at the end of this
huge pool to the Shallows. Beyond them
I imagine I can see the pinky coral spires
of Shark Point glittering. Our home.

I swish my tail like never before.

Brrrrrrrrrrrrrrrrrrrm-mmmmmmmmmmmmm!!!

I have no idea what that noise is. But it's not going to put us off.

I fin my fins like it's the last time I will ever fin them.

The water is bursting in my gills.

My mouth is open.

My hammer is down.

Brrrrrrrrrrrrrrrrrrrrrrm-mmmmmmmmmmmm!!!!

Nope. Nothing is going to distract us!!!

I rush for the surface, breaking through the waves and leaping into the air. Escape, here I come!

Whee!!!

Brrrrrrrrrrrrrrrrrrrmmm. Click.
Hissssssssssssssssss.

Bang!!!

Flappp!!!

Crunch!!!

Splash!!!

What????? I'm back in the pool.

How? Why?

A second later Rick lands beside me.

Crasssssssssshhhhhhhhhhh.

Just as winded. Just as annoyed.

We look at each other, then up and up and up and *up.*

Oh. My. Cod.

I can't believe my googly hammer eyes! There's a huge clear-plastic wall reaching yards and yards into the air! It's risen on some sort of mechanism from *behind* the wall I thought we were able to jump over.

That's what the distracting *brrrrrrrrr-rrrrrrrrrrmmm, click, hissssssssss* had been! The see-through wall coming up from below!!!!!

"Busted. Totally busted, kid."

Thanks, Mike. I hadn't noticed.

"Well done, pick-ax brain!" Rick yells at me. "Not only have you come up with the ocean's all-time stupidest plan, but you've shown the leggy air-breathers that we can do better tricks than the dolphins, so now they're going to make us perform for them *for the rest of our lives!!!!!!!!!!!!!!!!!!!!!!!!*"

CHAPTER 6

I search my head for some advice from Imaginary Mike Hammerhead.

"I have nothing, kid, you're on your own."

Thanks, Imaginary Mike. That really helps!

I swim slowly around Rick, scratching

my hammer in total frustration.

Rick floats motionless in the perfor-mance pool, nose down.

I think I see a tear in his eye.

Rick quickly fins it away, and any sign of weakness is gone.

"You got us into this," he says with a low-down snarly growl. "You get us out!"

There's no point telling him that I wouldn't be here at all if it wasn't for him swimming away from home to join the sea-circus, and me finding his stupid jacket and coming to save him.

There's no point telling him but it doesn't stop me *thinking* it.

I widen my circle.

Come on Imaginary Mike Hammerhead, Shark Detective, you've been in tighter spots than this. Help me out, here! I search my brain for ideas but all I get is:

"••• ••• ••• • •   ••• ••• ••• ••• •••   ••• ••• ••• ••• ••• ••• ••• ••• • •   ••• ••• ••• ••• ••• ••• ••• ••• ••• ••• • •

••• ••• ••• ••• ••• •"

I guess I really am on my own.

Ping!

What?

Ping! Ping! Pinnnnnnnngg!!!!!

My hammer-vision has suddenly turned itself on. Now, this only happens for a very small number of reasons.

There's food nearby.

There's danger nearby.

That's it.

There's certainly no food in the performance pool and Rick is not my idea of lunch, so it *must* be danger.

I narrow my eyes. It's time for Harry Hammer to become *Harry Hammer, Shark Detective* for real. No more Mr. Nice Shark.

I scan the immediate area with my hammer-vision on *maximum*.

Danger can come in many forms. I can see that only Rick and I are in the pool. So it can't be any leggy air-breathers. It must be something else.

I swim down, and my hammer-vision starts going crazy.

Ping ping hiss ping ping ping!!!!!

The *pings* are dragging my hammer around toward the wall of the pool. The *hiss ping* narrows it down. I swim over, not knowing what to expect.

"What are you doing, kelp breath?" Rick calls to me.

I ignore him.

Harry Hammer, Shark Detective is on the case.

I reach the wall and start up hammer-vision-scan-mode-*ultra*. The wall zooms into sharp focus.

"In the mean performance pool," I drawl to myself like Mike Hammerhead, "you have to pay the closest of attention. Every clue counts."

Yes!

There!

Right where the wall turns a corner to head back toward the shore, is a crack that I didn't notice before. It's not a big crack, but it is slowly bulging out from the weight of the water it's holding in the pool.

I swim closer.

Where the tide has gone out beyond the shore, there's no longer equal pressure from sea to hold it up. The whole thing is in danger of collapsing!

I tap it with my hammer.

Nothing.

I thud it with my hammer.

Ping ping ping hisssssssssssssssss-ssssssssssss!!!!

The crack splits a little farther up the wall. . . .

I swim back to Rick, my heart pounding with excitement. This time I don't hug him. But I do whisper in his ear.

"Rick. I have *another* plan!"

Minutes later we're putting on the best show the leggy air-breathers have *ever seen*!! And if my new plan works, they'll never see anything like it ever again!! Or at least they better not.

I pull a three-sixty hammer-dart and tail-rush down to the weak spot in the wall.

The crowd cheers and goes wild. Their excited yelling and clapping completely covers up the sound of me *thumping* my hammer at full speed on to the crack!

Tsssssskkkkkk! (That's the crack, cracking open a little bit more!)

Rick runs a shallow-half-wave-roll-flip and plunges down.

Cheers!!! Yells!!!! Applause!!!!!!

Thump!!!! Rick bangs the crack with his nose.

TsssSSSSSSSSSSsskkkkkk!!!!! It opens up a little more.

I drop a totally awesome seven-tail

and Acrosprat devil-dive and *thump* the crack with my hammer.

TsssSSSSSSSSsssssssssssssssssssSSS-SSSSSSSSSSSSSSSSSSSSSSSSssskkkkkk!!!!!

"Harry, it's working!" Rick yells as we swim past each other.

I nod my hammer. "Just continue on!"

Rick powers out of the water, turns a ninety-degree jaw-dog, back-splashes into three-and-a-half gill-jumps, and crashes into the water in a furious-shark-dart.

Cheers!!! Yells!!!! Applause!!!!!!

Thump!!!!

TsssSSSSSSSSsssssssssssssssssssSSS-SSSSSSSSSSSSSSSSSSSSSSSSssskkkkkk!!!!!

I race a radical side-fin to the other end of the pool, turn, and just kick it!

Just like the super-sharktastic detective secret agent I am. Right, Mike?

I'm swimming on all muscles. Every system is *go*. I'm scything through the water like a speed shark. I'm heading to pull the biggest trick of my life. As I leap into the totally awesomest hammer-flick and seven-twenty-degree heart-stopper with tail-splash, I yell, "Sometimes justice is left to *just us*!!!!!"

"Never a truer word spoken, kid. Go get 'em like a pro!"

Thanks, Imaginary Mike! I couldn't have done it without you!

"Oh yes, you could!"

Cheers!!! Yells!!!! Applause!!!!!!

I dive under the water and ram my hammer into the crack.

Thump!!!

TsssSSSSSSSSsssssssssssssssssSSS-SSSSSSSSSSSSSSSSSsskkkkKKKKKKKK!!!!!

Booooooooooooom!!!

Ker-smash!!!!!!!!

Whoooooooooooooooooooooshhh!!!

The crowd goes silent as the wall cracks *open*!!

The water rushes through as the plastic is torn apart by the pressure.

"Hold my fin, Rick!" I yell. "This is gonna be *radical*!!!"

I grab hold of Rick's fin, and he grabs mine. We're washed out of the pool,

riding a huge wave of released water straight out to where the tide is!

"Yay!" shouts Rick.

"We've done it, Rick! We've flippering done it!!!"

It's almost like we're Acrosprats!

We're free. We've escaped! We're back in the Shallows and now we can finally go home.

But not before we both pull the biggest and best nose-swivel, gill-gimbal, and a totally fantastic screwball-dorsal-bump for the crowd of openmouthed, completely silent, and shocked leggy air-breathers!!!!

Those finless, air-breathing wonders had no idea who they were dealing with when they messed with Rick and me. Well, mainly me.

Fin-pump!!!!!!!

CHAPTER 7

As soon as Rick and I swim out of the Shallows and start making our way back toward the center of Shark Point, I notice something really weird.

The roads are totally empty. Even though it's Saturday, there are no whalebuses, tunatrucks, or taxicrabs to be seen. There are no families coming into town to do their shopping. And the shark-parks are empty, the swings bumping lazily against themselves in the currents. But the weirdest thing of all is the silence.

The great feeling of escaping from the performance pool has been replaced by a bubbly scaredy feeling in my tummy. I know what it's like to be Joe the Bottom-Popping Jellyfish all over again.

Pop.

Don't tell anyone, okay?

"I don't like it," says Rick.

"I don't like it either," I say.

We swim on.

My street is completely deserted too. The mayor's residence, my home, is locked up and it doesn't matter how many times I fin on the door, it doesn't open.

The same happens at Rick's house.

This is so weird.

I fire up my hammer-vision and crank it right up to *ultra-plus.*

Ping! Ping! Ping! Ping! Ping! Ping!

Hmm. It's a tiny response. I zero in on the direction of the *ping.*

Ping! Ping! Ping! Ping! Ping! Ping!

Zooming in even more, to way off into the distance, I can see something floppy and messy.

I immediately recognize it.

And get sick to my stomach.

It's my *dad's* floppy, messy hair! It's waving around in the distance, just above the buildings between us and the town square. And judging by the way his hair is flopping and waving and swirling in the currents, I'd say Dad is pretty agitated.

But at least my hammer-vision has told me where he is.

"There's my dad!" I shout to Rick, who's still looking sadly through the windows of his house. "Let's go!"

We start swimming toward the town square.

"I applaud all the citizens of Shark Point for pulling together in our time of need.

I can hear Dad before I can see him—from *three* streets away.

He has his mayoral megaphone out and his voice is booming through the water.

"My hero was my grandfather Harrington Hammer. Let me tell you a story. . . ."

As we swim closer I hear the murmuring of voices and as we turn the last corner, I see the reason that Shark Point seems completely deserted.

Everyone is here! The square is full of moms, dads, kids, squids, clams, and crabs! They're all listening intently to Dad as he makes an idiot of himself. *As usual!*

Dad is strutting up and down outside the building with his megaphone clasped tightly in his fin, floppy hair waving crazily in the currents from his excited tail. Mom is floating next to him looking really concerned.

Dad puts the megaphone back to his mouth to address the huge crowd.

"Harry and Rick have been missing for many hours, and it is our duty to

find them!" He clears his throat and gets really serious. "We shall search for them on the seas and oceans, we shall search for them with growing confidence, and growing strength in the water, we shall search for them on the beaches, we shall search for them on the spawning grounds, we shall search on the seafloor and the streets, we shall never surrender, this will be our fin-est hour!!!"

Mom finbows him in the side.

Dad coughs. "Yes, well, what I'm trying to say is that I want volunteer teams of our fastest and best sharks to form search parties to head out right now and search for my son, Harry, and his best friend, Rick!"

Best friend? *Dad!*

Rick says nothing but I can see he has that smirky look on his face. I float out of *flubbering* range just in case.

"This is an emergency," Dad continues, "and although there is not a moment to lose, I would just like to say that I am also reminded of my great-grandfather Harrison Hammer, who . . ."

I have to put a stop to this. It's more embarrassing than Mom spitting on her hanky to wipe bits of Kelp-Krispies off my lips at the school gates *in front of everyone.*

Why do moms do that, by the way?!

Anyway, I have to put a stop to this *now*.

As everyone in the square is look-ing up at Dad and not at me and Rick, we swim right up to the front of the town hall before anyone notices. I tug on Dad's fin.

"Dad! It's us. We're back!"

"Not now, Harry! Can't you see I'm busy trying to organize a search party?"

"Who for?"

"For you and Rick of course! Now will you please stop interrupting! As I was saying, I'm reminded of my great-grandfather Harrison Hammer, who once got lost in the wilderness beyond the shelf for three and a half weeks, while prospecting for whelks. He was only able to survive by eating whatever he could find from under rocks! To think that Harry, here, might—"

I tug harder on his fin and flick his dorsal with my hammer.

"Harry! For goodness' sake, I'm trying to get these people to go out and find you!"

He swings back around, puts the megaphone back to his mouth, and . . .

Clang!!!!

(That's the sound of his brain finally figuring out that I don't need rescuing.)

"Harry!" Dad yells. *"And Rick! You're back!"*

"Yes, Dad, we are!" I snap. "So can you please stop shouting through the megaphone?!"

The next few minutes are a blur of cheering and hugging—and trying to avoid Mom spitting on her handkerchief to wipe a smudge of sea-sand off my face.

When things finally start to calm down, and Rick's parents have come over to give him a cuddle, Mom asks me what happened.

But before I can open my jaws, Rick blurts, "I was captured by the leggy air-breathers and held prisoner inside their Sea-Planet Theme Park. It was terrible, and then they captured Harry and he was terrified. I thought it would be a good idea to trick them into letting us in the pool nearest the sea and then I decided that we'd break through the wall and escape and here we are. Easy!"

The lies tumble out of Rick's mouth like pops from Joe's bottom!

I look at Rick with eyes wider than the Mariana Trench (which is very wide—poolgle it on your computers and see).

I think Mom and Dad can tell from my face that I can't believe what Rick's saying. Mom whispers something in Dad's ear. He nods and picks up the megaphone again. . . .

Oh no!

"Dad! No!" I start waving my fins at him

127

to stop, expecting him to say something totally embarrassing again. But he doesn't. He just asks, "What about you, Harry? How did you get mixed up in this?"

"At the end of the day, Harry, on the mean streets we only need one weapon, our wits and a good old hard dose of truth."

That's two weapons, Imaginary Mike, but thank you for pointing out what I need to do. I take the megaphone from my dad.

"Math was never my strong point, kid. You go get 'em, Harry Hammer, Super Agent Shark Detective: Instrument of Truth, Justice, and the Hammerhead Way!"

I take a deep gill of water and start speaking into the megaphone. "The truth is I went looking for Rick when I found his jacket on a rock in the Shallows. I know how much he loves that jacket and he would never have left it behind unless he was forced to. I knew he had to be in danger—so I continued on into the Shallows alone."

The crowd gasps. Everyone looks at Rick. He grudgingly nods. The crowd gasps again.

"And that's when I was captured," I continue. "But I came up with a plan to get us out—inspired by my great hero"—Dad puffs his chest up with pride—"Mike Hammerhead, Shark Detective." Dad's puffy chest deflates like a burst balloon. "It was my idea to put on a show for the leggy air-breathers so we'd get put in the pool right next to the ocean. Then I saw a crack in the wall of the pool with my hammer-vision, so we pounded the crack during our show until the wall

130

broke and we could escape. And we escaped in the finest display of sea acrospratics the ocean has ever seen."

The crowd double gasps. Everyone looks at Rick again. He double grudgingly nods. The crowd double gasps again.

"Hooray for *Harry!*"

Everyone is hugging us and cheering again. Tony, Ralph (looking hungrily into my mouth to make up for his missed meals), and Joe appear from the crowd. Tony and Ralph swim up and down waving their fins like victory flags in the current.

But Joe starts mumbling in my ear.

"I'm so glad you weren't turned into shark-fin soup for leggy air-breathers to suck up through straws. I'm so glad your hides weren't turned into shoes, because imagine how rawful it would be having stinky leggy air-breather's weird-shaped feet inside you all day. And I'm so glad your teeth weren't turned into necklaces for leggy air-breather's to—"

I put a fin over Joe's mouth.

His bottom instantly starts to pop.

"Can't you just be glad we're home?" I say with a grin.

"I am," says Joe. "Let's hope you don't

get run over by a whalebus or a taxi-crab though. That would be a horrible welcome home."

I start to giggle. "You'll never change, will you, Joe?"

Joe waves his tentacles in horror. "No! Changing is really scary!"

Laughing, I swim away to join the celebrations.

I feel awesome! Not only have I solved my first proper mystery, but Rick has had to admit that *I* was the real hero who saved *him*. Hopefully, I might avoid a few *flubbers* over the next few weeks at school. After all,

Rick totally wouldn't want to get caught *flubbering* the shark who saved his life: *Harry Hammer, Shark Detective: Instrument of Truth, Justice, and the Hammerhead Way!!!*

THE END

Meet Harry and the Shark Point gang. . . .

HARRY

Species:

hammerhead shark

You'll spot him . . .

using his special

hammer-vision

Favorite thing:

his Gregor the Gnasher

poster

Most likely to say:

"I wish I was a great white."

Most embarrassing moment: when Mom called him

her "little starfish" in front of all his friends

RALPH

Species:

pilot fish

You'll spot him . . .

eating the food from

between Harry's teeth!

Favorite thing: shrimp Pop-Tarts

Most likely to say: "So, Harry, what's for

breakfast today?"

Most embarrassing moment: eating too much cake

on Joe's birthday. His face was COVERED in pink

plankton icing.

JOE

Species: jellyfish

You'll spot him . . . hiding behind
Ralph and Harry, or behind his
own tentacles

Favorite thing: his cave, since it's
nice and safe

Most likely to say: "If we do this,
we're going to end up as
fish food. . . ."

Most embarrassing moment:
whenever his rear goes *toot*, which is when
he's scared. Which is all the time.

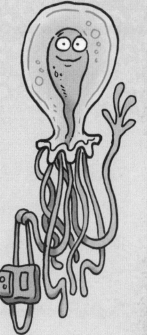

RICK

Species: blacktip reef shark

You'll spot him . . .

bullying smaller fish

or showing off

Favorite thing: his black

leather jacket

Most likely to say:

"Last one there's a sea snail!"

Most embarrassing moment:

none. Rick's far too cool to get embarrassed.